P9-EKX-010

See Santa Nap

story and pictures by
DAVID MILGRIM

Atheneum Books for Young Readers
New York London Toronto Sydney

For Lenny, Karina, Celia, and Marc

Atheneum Books for Young Readers • An imprint of Simon & Schuster Children's Publishing Division
1230 Avenue of the Americas • New York, New York 10020 • Copyright © 2004 by David Milgrim
All rights reserved, including the right of reproduction in whole or in part in any form.
Book design by Sonia Chaghatzbanian • The text for this book is set in Century OldStyle.
The illustrations are rendered in digital pen-and-ink. • Manufactured in the United States of America
First Edition • 1 2 3 4 5 6 7 8 9 10 • Library of Congress Cataloging-in-Publication Data
Milgrim, David. • See Santa nap / David Milgrim.—1st ed. • p. cm.— (The adventures of Otto)
Summary: After delivering presents, Santa needs a nap, but Otto and his friends like their gifts so much
that Santa cannot find a quiet place to sleep. • ISBN 0-689-85928-7
[1. Santa Claus—Fiction. 2. Naps (Sleep)—Fiction. 3. Noise—Fiction. 4. Robots—Fiction. 5. Animals—Fiction.]
I. Title. II. Series: Milgrim, David. Adventures of Otto. • PZ7 .M5955Se 2004 • [E]—dc22 2003022937

See Santa.
See Santa give.

Give, Santa, give.

See Santa
give his last
two gifts.

Now Santa is all done.
See Santa nap.
Nap, Santa, nap.

See Flop.
See Flop's new drum.
Thank you, Santa!

See Santa
nap again.

Look, Pip got a
new water gun!
Thank you, Santa!

See Santa nap
one more time.

Look, Wally got
a new ball!
Thank you, Santa!

See Santa nap at last.

See Peanut.
See Peanut's new swimsuit.
Look out, Santa!

Uh-oh, there goes Santa!

See Santa get
no rest at all.

Look, Otto got a fishing pole!
Go, Otto, go!

See Otto save Santa!
Yay, Otto!

Uh-oh, where is Santa going now?

Look, Santa is in
Otto's tree house!
Thank you, Otto.

See Santa nap.

Nap, Santa, nap.